MODERN STORIES

HISTORIC TALES

General Editors:
Wendy Body   Pat Edwards   Margarette Thomas-Cochran

LONGMAN

A Note to the Reader

What makes for historical fiction?

It is quite straight forward. The stories are set in the past. They often deal with past events that may have really taken place, but they're written today.

To write a good piece of **historical fiction**, the author has to paint a realistic picture of what life was like. To do this, he or she has to do a lot of research. The setting must be real even if the characters aren't.

You can have a lot of fun with **historical fiction**. If you were the author, you could choose to weave yourself into a story that takes place three hundred years ago! Try it sometime!

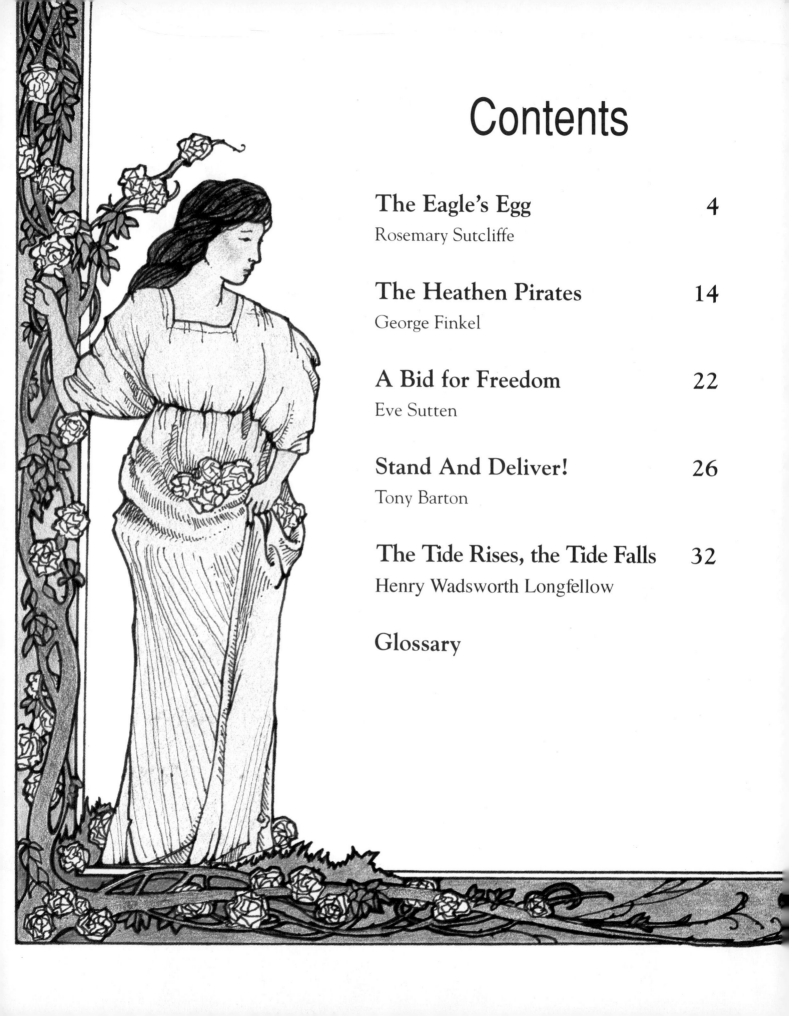

Contents

THE EAGLE'S EGG

Quintus is a young Standard-bearer with the Ninth Legion stationed at Eburacum (York) in second-century Roman Britain. At this time the eagle standard was used by all Roman legions throughout the empire. The Standard-bearer marched at the head of the foot soldiers, carrying this symbol of Rome's power and glory, and Quintus was proud of his rank. But now he needs to gain promotion to centurion, for only centurions are allowed to marry, and Quintus has fallen in love with Cordaella, a British girl. It seems he must earn it the hard way, by serving in one of General Agricola's campaigns to subdue the Painted People in the wilds of Calidonia (Scotland). But there has been no word of a campaign and even the discovery that Vedrix, Cordaella's brother, will not stand in their way, does not solve the problem. Until one day . . .

I was standing before the piled writing-table in the Headquarters Office, where Dexius Valens the Senior Centurion had sent for me, waiting for him to notice that I was there. After a while he looked up from the scatter of tablets and papyrus rolls before him, and said, "Ah, Standard-bearer. — Yes, the General Agricola is at Corstopitum over-seeing the arrangements for this summer's Caledonian Campaign. The order has just come through. We march to join him in three days."

So that was that. All town leave was stopped, of course, and I never even got to see Cordaella to say farewell to her. Couldn't write her a note, either, because of course she couldn't read anyway. The best I could do was to scratch a few lines to Vedrix and ask him to read them to her — I thought I could trust him — and get one of the mule-drivers to take the letter down into the town the next day.

And three days later, leaving the usual holding-garrison behind us, we marched out for Corstopitum.

A Legion on the march — that's something worth the seeing; the long winding column, cohort after cohort, the cavalry wings spread on either side and the baggage train following after. A great serpent of mailed men, red-hackled with the crests of the officers' helmets, and whistling whatever tune best pleases them at the moment — "Payday" perhaps, or "The Emperor's Wineskins", or "The Girl I kissed at Clusium", to keep the marching time. Four miles to the hour, never slower, never faster, uphill and down, twenty miles a day .... And me, marching up at the head, right behind the Legate on his white horse, carrying the great Eagle of the Legion, with the sunlight splintering on its spread wings; and its talons clutched on the lighting-jags of Jupiter, and the gilded laurel wreaths of its victories ....

Aye, I was the proud one, that day! For I'd seen Cordaella among the crowd that gathered to see us off, and she had seen me and waved to me. And I was through with garrison duty and going to join the fighting, and win my promotion and maybe make a name for myself and come back with the honours shining on my breast; and all for my girl Cordaella. And my breast swelled as though the honours were already there. What a bairn I was, what a boy with my head chock-full of dreams of glory, for all the great lion-skin that I wore over my armour, and the size of my hands on the Eagle shaft, and my long legs eating up the Northward miles!

But it was three years and more before we came marching back; and there were times when I came near to forgetting Cordaella for a while, though never quite.

We joined Agricola with the Twentieth Legion at Corstopitum, and marched on North across the great Lowland hills until we were

joined by the main part of the Second and the Fourteenth that had come up through the western country of last summer's campaigning.

Then we headed on for the broad Firth that all but cuts Caledonia in half. The Fleet met us there, and we spent the rest of the summer making a naval base. You need something of that sort for supplies, and support, when you can't be sure of your land lines of communication behind you. We saw a bit of fighting from time to time, but seemingly the Lowland chiefs were still too busy fighting with each other, to make a strong show against us, so mostly it was just building; first the supply base, and then with the winter scarce past, a string of turf and timber forts right across the low-lying narrows of the land.

Sick and tired we got of it, too, and there began to be a good deal of grumbling. I mind Lucius, a mate of mine growling into his supper bannock that he might as well have stayed at home and been a builder's labourer — and me trying to give him the wink that the Cohort Commander was standing right behind him. It's odd, the small daft things not worth remembering, that one remembers across half a lifetime . . .

But in the next spring, when we started the big push on into the Highlands, we found a difference.

Somehow, sometime in that second winter, the Caledonians had found the leader they needed to hammer them into one people. Calgacus, his name was, I never saw him, not until the last battle; but I got so that the bare mention of his name would have me looking over my shoulder and reaching for my sword. It was the same with all of us, especially when the mists came down from the high tops or rain blotted out the bleak country as far as a man could see. Oh yes, we saw plenty enough fighting that summer, to make up for any breathing space we'd had in the two before.

Agricola was too cunning a fox to go thrusting his muzzle up into the mountains, with every turf of bog-cotton seemingly a war-painted warrior in disguise, waiting to close the glens like a trap on his tail. Instead, he closed them himself, with great forts in the mouths of each one where it came down to the eastern plain. That way, there was no risk of the tribes swarming down unchecked to take us in the rear or cut our supply lines afer we had passed by.

We got sullen-sick of fort building, all over again, yes; especially with our shoulder-blades always on the twitch for an arrow between them. The Ninth wintered at Inchtuthil, the biggest of the forts. The place was not finished, but we sat in the middle and went on building it round us, which is never a very comfortable state of things, in enemy country. We lost a lot of men in one way and another; and the old ugly talk of the Ninth being an unlucky Legion woke up and began to drift round again.

It might have been better if the Legate had not had a convenient bout of stomach trouble and gone south to winter in Corstopitum. I didn't envy Senior Centurion Dexius left in command. It was our third winter in the wilds, and we were sick of snow and hill mists, and the painted devils sniping at us from behind every gorse-bush; and we wanted to be able to drink with our friends in a wine shop, and walk twenty paces without wondering what was coming up behind us. And we cursed the Legate for being comfortable in Corstopitum, and grew to hate the sight of each other's faces.

I began to smell trouble coming, sure as acorns grow on oak trees.

And then one day when we had almost won through to spring, some of the men broke into the wine store and were found drunk on watch. They were put under guard, ready to be brought up before the Senior Centurion next day. And everyone knew what that meant. He'd have been within his rights to order the death penalty; but being Daddy Dexius, who could be relied on to be soft in such matters, they would probably get off with a flogging. Even so, it would be the kind of flogging that spreads a man flat on his face in the sick block for three days afterwards.

All the rest of that day you could feel the trouble like nearing thunder prickling in the back of your neck. And in the middle of supper, it came.

Being the Eagle bearer, I ate in the Centurions' mess-hall, though in the lowest place there, next to the door; and I hadn't long sat down when the noise began.

It wasn't particularly loud, but there was an ugly note to it; a snarling note; and in the midst of it someone shouting, "Come on, lads, let's get the prisoners out!" and other voices taking up the cry.

I remember Dexius's face as he got up and strode past me to the door; and suddenly knowing that we had all been quite wrong about him; that he wasn't soft at all. More the kind of man who gets a reputation for being good-tempered and fair-game, because he knows that if he once lets his temper go and hits somebody he probably won't leave off till he's killed them.

I had only just started my supper, so I snatched a hard-boiled duck's egg from a bowl on the table and shoved it down the front of my uniform, and dashed out with the rest.

Outside on the parade-ground a crowd was gathering. Some of them had makeshift torches. The flare of them was teased by the thin wind that was blowing, and their light fell ragged on faces that were sullen and dangerous. Vipsanius the duty centurion was trying to deal with the situation, but he didn't seem to be having much success, and the crowd was getting bigger every moment.

Daddy Dexius said coolly, "What goes on here, Centurion?"

"They're refusing to go on watch, Sir," said Vipsanius. I mind he was sweating up a bit, despite the edge to the wind.

"We've had enough of going on watch in this dog-hole, night after filthy night!" someone shouted.

And his mates backed him up. "How much longer are we going to squat here, making a free target of ourselves for the blue painted barbarians?"

"If Agricola wants to fight them, why doesn't he come up and get things going?"

"Otherwise why don't we get out of here and go back where we came from?"

Men began shouting from all over the crowd, bringing up all the old soldiers' grievances about pay and leave and living conditions. "We've had enough!" they shouted, "We've had enough!"

"You'll have had more than enough, and the Painted People down on us, if you don't break up and get back on duty!" Vipsanius yelled back at them.

The Heathen Pirates

Lucius Bedwyr Marcianus, who lives in the north of Britain, is of Roman ancestry and his family are rich, owning many sheep and cattle. He is called 'lord', even though he is only a young teenager. Long ago, his grandfather had been named king of the area and now his father rules over the community of around ten thousand. Their people are Christian and despise the heathen pirates who sweep down in raids from the far north to pillage and rape the small coastal settlements. The time is around 500 A.D.

Bedwyr (as he is called) is delighted when his father gives permission for him to take the kegs of honey ale to the outlying shepherds to help them celebrate the Feast of Saint Alban. With him is Katti, his best friend. Katti, a soldier originally from West Britain, is some years older than Bedwyr. Before leaving they collect a five-foot bore spear and a full quiver of arrows from Zaal, the community smith.

Gwenyfer, Bedwyr's cousin, is also in her early teens. She sneaks out to join the party despite orders that she should stay at home. It is she who suggests they should leave the pack train and climb Tor Magma, the great jutting mass of the uplands.

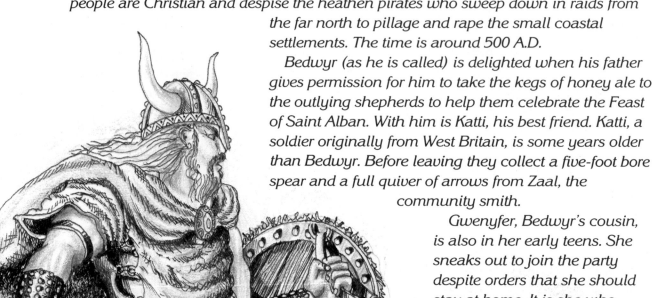

We ate our midday meal before we went on — it seemed foolish to carry the food to the top, adding to our burden — and then continued on foot and unshod, our footgear slung by their straps round our necks. We climbed noiselessly, perhaps breathing a little harder than usual, but our breathlessness prevented speech. As things turned out, this was perhaps just as well.

There was no track as the slope grew steeper, and we gradually strung out in single file. I was first, being nimbler on my feet than Katti, while my cousin was behind him again, hampered in her climbing by her gown. The last twenty feet or so to the top of the Tor rose steeply, becoming almost a little grass-grown cliff; I had to use my hands to help me climb it, pulling myself up by grasping firmly rooted grass tufts. I reached the top and looked over the edge, and almost cried out at what I saw.

Across the little plateau, not forty feet away, stood a thick-set figure gazing up-river. He wore woollen breeches, cross-gartered, and clumsy shoes of untanned hide, while a leather jerkin clothed his upper body. On his head he wore a leather helmet with an ox-horn set on either side of it. Two other men were clumsily scrambling over the far side of the summit close to him. Although I had never seen one before, I knew well enough what they were: heathen pirates!

All this I saw as I clung there, my feet on an insecure hold of grass-tufts and only the upper part of my head over the ridge. It looked as if the first heathen — the standing one — had himself only just arrived on the crest, and was very naturally looking back the way he had come. Had he been there only a little earlier he would no doubt have come to look in the other direction, and seen us, utterly defenceless, struggling up the slope.

At any moment he might turn, and I would be seen, or one of his struggling followers might see my head outlined against the sky. My heart beat a strong pulse and my throat was dry, but I was not conscious of any fear. Silently I let go of my handhold and slid backwards the way I had come, contriving to gesture Katti to silence as I went past him.

Forty feet below the crest was a clump of bracken, and behind this we lay flat, my cousin between us. We had gestured her to silence also, and she lay between us, puzzled but unafraid. She has always been as good or better than a man in any crisis.

"What's amiss, lord? Did you see something on the top?"

Though Katti kept his voice low, it still sounded over-loud to me.

"I saw three heathen pirates," I said. "One on his feet by the farther edge, and two just breasting the ridge beside him."

"How did you know they were heathen and not some of our own people?"

I described the men's appearance and dress in as few words as I could.

"Did you see anything — a pattern, a device, something coloured — on the front of the leader's jerkin?"

"There was something there, blue-coloured, but I did not see what it was."

Katti nodded. "That would be right — it would be his chief's token, perhaps his own if he were a high man among them." He unslung his bow, and rolled over on his back to string it. When he had done this he rolled forwards again. "Lord, listen well. These men will not be alone, and they must not escape." He looked keenly about. I could tell he was thinking of a plan. "You see that rock over there?"

He pointed past me to a flat tilted slab, one edge level with the ground and the lower part two feet above the surface. I nodded, wondering what was in his mind.

"Cross over to it, then crouch behind it, unslinging your spear. There are loose stones on the ground. Pick a good-sized one, and fling it to the top of the Tor. You can do that, lord?"

I nodded. "And then what?"

"I think they will come over to see where the stone came from. I will get one, perhaps two, with arrows as they look. If I get the horned one, and perhaps one of the others, I think the third will run back the way he came. I can deal with him later. But after you have flung the stone, keep well down. You have no helmet, and they are very good at casting a knife or hatchet."

"And I, Katti?"

"You will stay here, lady. In your green gown you will not be seen in this bracken. Now, lord — go!"

As I crouched and ran for the shelter of the rock to the right, Katti rose and moved to the left, standing up and making no attempt at concealment. He drew three arrows from the quiver, sticking two loosely into the turf in front of him and setting the third on the bowstring. I gained the rock, unslung the spear, and took up a large stone.

My first cast was a failure — I had taken too large a stone, and tried to fling it while kneeling. I took another, stood up, and contrived to lob it over the crest. Then I dropped back behind my rock, but could not resist looking round the edge of it to see what was going to happen.

The results were almost immediate. The horned man strode almost to the edge — and Katti's first arrow took him through the neck from side to side. He fell forward, sliding head-foremost down the steep slope, kicking and gurgling. Twenty feet down his head butted into a rock, and he reared uppermost, almost standing on his head. There was a sharp cracking noise, and he fell back, his limbs twitching. Later we found his neck was broken, although Katti's arrow alone would have killed him.

Not seeing the arrow, his two companions probably thought the edge had crumbled under him, and they sprang back so that I could only see them from the waist up. These seemed to be of a meaner sort than the horned man; their helmets had no ox-horns and their clothing bore no ornament. They were short and thick-set, wearing no beard, with long drooping moustaches. In appearance they were both repulsive and barbarous.

They did not see Katti until he called, a wordless cry, blood-curdling and fierce. As they turned, Katti's second arrow took one of the men in the left eye. He screamed, and plucked at it, trying to draw it out. This was a useless thing to do, had he but known it. Zaal's hunting arrows were so well barbed that they had either to be cut out, or driven right through. While he was riving at it, Katti's third arrow took him through the throat, front to back, pinning his arm to his neck. He dropped, and the screaming stopped.

While Katti plucked a fourth arrow from the quiver at his back, the third man did an unexpected thing. He could not have seen me, but he sprang over the edge of the Tor and came down the slope in giant strides straight at my rock, at the same time plucking a hatchet from his girdle to throw at Katti. His intention was obvious, and even if he missed his throw, he would be a difficult mark to hit going at speed down the hillside.

I do not think he even saw me, at least until it was too late to change his direction. The spearbutt was well bedded down, and I had a firm grip. At the last moment he may have seen the spear head and tried to leap aside, but it was too late — it took him where I intended, in the upper belly, just below the rib-cage. The long blade sank into his body right up to the cross-guard, and the impetus of his weight sank the spearbutt deep into the turf. He fell on top of me, pinning me down behind the rock, the hatchet flying from his dead hand as he fell.

He stank vilely, of unwashed body and foul woollen clothing. I lay beneath him, his body twitching and stirring on top of me, but only for a very short time. Then the body — for he was dead enough, the spearhead had broken his back — was heaved to one side, and Katti helped me to my feet. I leaned against the rock, gasping for breath.

"You are not hurt, lord?"

I nodded, not having breath to speak. Katti put his foot against the belly of my victim and dragged out the spear. The barbs below the head made a tearing sound as he cleared them. I looked at the bloody corpse, and laughed in a silly fashion, until Katti silenced me with a gesture.

"Your first heathen, lord — you have slain at an earlier age than I did. No one could say that you are not well-blooded, either."

There was a great patch of wet blood on the front of my tunic — the dead man's blood. I touched it, fascinated — the slimy feel of it on the well-woven wool of the tunic was horrible. I felt suddenly sick.

"Steady, lord. Put your head down between your knees — that's the way. There were but the three of them, and it's all over for the time being. Sit quiet for awhile."

Presently the blood flowed into my head again, my sight cleared, and I felt better. Katti took handfuls of bracken leaves and rubbed much of the blood from my tunic. Then we went over to where Gwenyfer still hid in the bracken. She cried out when she saw my bloody tunic.

"You are hurt, cousin!"

"Not I. This is heathen blood. I took the third one in the belly with the boar-spear, and he fell on me. That is all." I controlled my voice with an effort, finding I had a tendency to speak over-loudly.

"Oh, horrible!" she said. Then: "I have never seen a heathen. What are they like?"

"No fit sight for you, lady," said Katti. "And as for seeing them, that can wait. We must try to find out where they are from, and what their numbers are. Be good enough to stay here, lady, until we come back."

"But but — the heathen — " she said, indicating the two tumbled corpses.

"Have no fear of them, lady — their teeth are drawn, they cannot bite you. Bide quietly here while the Lord Bedwyr and I spy out the land."

Without a word she seated herself with her back to the dead heathens, took a little comb from the pouch at her girdle and began to re-dress her hair. Then we walked over to the dead heathen leader and Katti cut his arrow free and cleaned the head carefully in a patch of soft turf, telling me to do the same with the ruddied spear-head.

"It is not that I care about my next foeman, lord," he said, "but I was taught this way, and there is good sense in it. Rotting blood or flesh breeds a strong poison, and a scratch from a dirty weapon brings such a death as I would not want the worst heathen to suffer. These must be scalded in a cauldron when we get back to Turris Alba, but until then clean turf is better than nothing."

George Finkel
Illustrated by Peter Schmidli

21

A Bid for Freedom

Sydney, 1840

Jamie Fenton has just arrived in Sydney. His dad is a doctor who decided to emigrate to Sydney when his wife and daughter (Jamie's mum and sister) died.

While his dad attends to some business, Jamie sets off to explore the new town of Sydney on his own.

It was a funny mixture, Sydney. The streets were broad, much broader than in the English towns I knew. Some of the buildings, like the Post Office and the Bank, were solid and impressive, built of stone, and there was a strangely shaped brick church. But mixed up among these were cottages made of wood and a kind of muddy plaster, years old. It must have rained in recent days because the rough red earth of the streets was churned into mud, and deep pot holes were filled with rusty looking water.

Along George Street there were men working to set the road to rights. A gang of about twelve men, all wielding picks and shovels, were levelling the pot holes, digging out the mud. A guard marched up and down behind them, a musket slung over one shoulder, and in his hand a cane or whip, I couldn't be sure which.

When I looked more closely, I saw that the men who were working were fastened together by stout iron chains, with iron shackles tightly gripping their ankles.

23

"Stop work, you lot!"

A powerful bay horse had cantered along the rough road. The uniformed young man on the horse's back bent down and held out a sheet of paper to the convicts' guard.

"Number 12! Drop your shovel!"

The guard stooped and turned a key in Number 12's shackles, and set him loose. The convict made a bid for freedom. He swung round and lurched a few desperate steps away from the guard. He never had a chance. In no time at all he was handcuffed, and fastened with a chain to the horse's bridle. Rider and guard exchanged rough salutes, and the convict, half running, half dragged, was on his way. Back to prison, I wondered, or to freedom?

I turned away, feeling a bit sick at what I'd seen. A sharp blow landed in my ribs, and I found myself in a heap on the ground, all tangled up with a boy of about my own age.

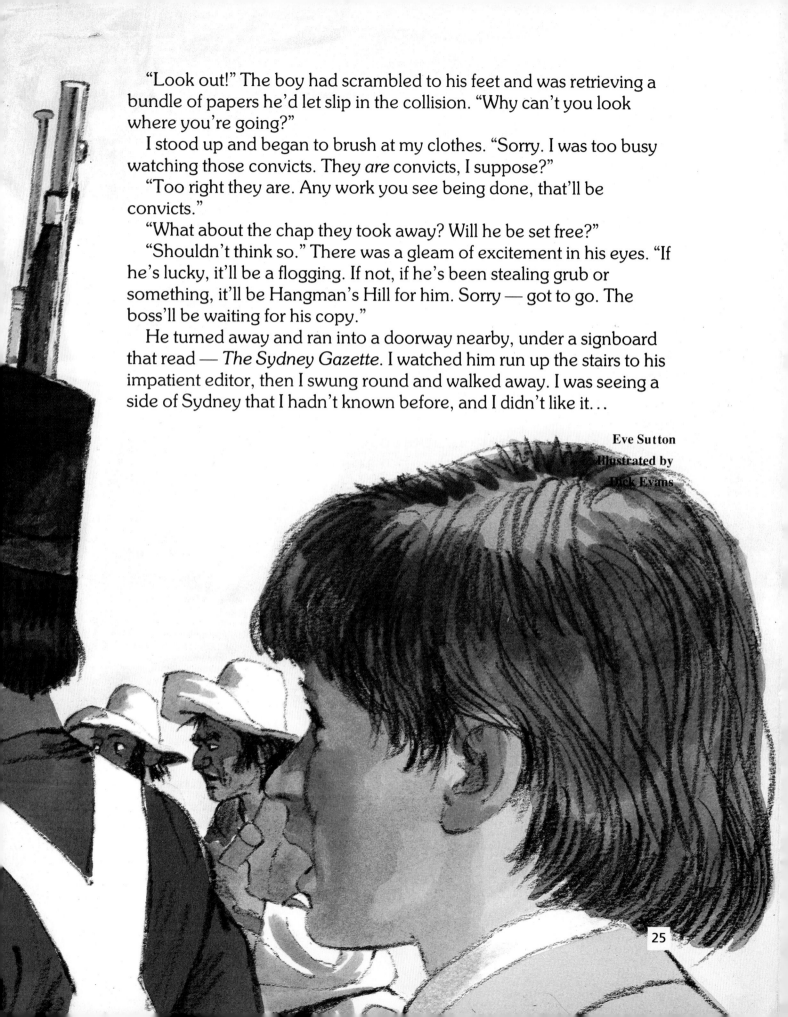

"Look out!" The boy had scrambled to his feet and was retrieving a bundle of papers he'd let slip in the collision. "Why can't you look where you're going?"

I stood up and began to brush at my clothes. "Sorry. I was too busy watching those convicts. They *are* convicts, I suppose?"

"Too right they are. Any work you see being done, that'll be convicts."

"What about the chap they took away? Will he be set free?"

"Shouldn't think so." There was a gleam of excitement in his eyes. "If he's lucky, it'll be a flogging. If not, if he's been stealing grub or something, it'll be Hangman's Hill for him. Sorry — got to go. The boss'll be waiting for his copy."

He turned away and ran into a doorway nearby, under a signboard that read — *The Sydney Gazette*. I watched him run up the stairs to his impatient editor, then I swung round and walked away. I was seeing a side of Sydney that I hadn't known before, and I didn't like it...

Eve Sutton

Illustrated by

Dick Evans

Stand and Deliver!

The year is 1737. The country is England. Peter Fletcher and his father, Simon, are about to travel from York to London to look for work. His father is carrying all the money they have, so they're nervous when they hear that Dick Turpin, the notorious highwayman, has been seen near their city of York .

Peter and his father climbed up onto the top of the London coach. It was cheaper to ride "outside".

As they drove down the Great North Road, Peter had a lot of time to think about Dick Turpin. "Was it Turpin who tried to stop that coach yesterday? Will he stop us? Will he be kind to us?"

But for three days, the coach drove through forests and fields and cities, stopping many times. They stopped at the inns, to change horses, and they stopped at all the turnpike gates to pay the toll. A man waited at each turnpike to open the gate and collect the money.

Then, as they got near London, they came to the Green Man Inn in Epping Forest. The horses were tired and new horses would be waiting at the inn.

Peter was tired too. There was nothing to do on the coach. All the way he had been sitting next to a big fat man who talked and talked and made him sleepy. The man's name was Mr Buffard, and he never stopped talking about his farm and all the things that he did there. Peter looked at his father, and he knew from his face that he, too, thought the fat man talked too much.

Peter got down to see the inn and the things that were happening there. Two men were taking the tired horses away from the coach.

"Hey, Walter!" shouted the coachman to one of these men. "Give me some good horses now — I hear Turpin was in the forest last night."

Walter called back, "No, someone's been telling you lies, my friend. Turpin was at Blackheath last night. He stopped a man and took all his money and his horse. People say Turpin gave him back his watch, because the man said it was a present from his dear old mother."

The other man said, "But Walter, if he was in Blackheath last night, he could be in Epping tonight. His horse Black Bess is the quickest in England."

"All right, Joe," answered Walter, "but we must stop talking. Mr Bayes will be angry if we don't get on with our work!"

There were people everywhere at the inn. People talking, people laughing, people eating and drinking. Peter heard bells ringing inside the inn, shouts for more drinks, men and women running everywhere.

He sat down by a wall, and looked through all the legs moving so quickly. He saw a small, rat-faced boy in poor clothes like himself. The boy ran about looking at people all the time. He looked for a long time at Mr Buffard. The fat man was still talking but not to Simon Fletcher now.

At last, Walter and Joe came back with the horses. Soon, everyone got into their places in the coach.

Peter looked down and saw the poor boy again. Now he was speaking quickly to a man Peter had not seen before. The man looked at a gold watch in his hand, and there was more gold on his blue coat and his black hat. A beautiful black horse stood beside this man, her nose on his arm. He looked at the coach as it went out of the inn.

Peter thought, "He's looking at me. Or is it Mr Buffard? I'd like to know who he is. He looks rich."

The man said something to the rat-faced boy, got on his horse, and rode away.

The coachman drove the horses out onto the highway, and they were soon going along through the trees towards London. The light was not good in the forest. In some parts, the trees grew near the road. A man could hide in these places.

There had been no rain and the road was good. All the time the coachman drove his horses hard. "I want to get out of the forest soon," he said.

Peter thought about the rat-faced boy, about working in London, about a man in a blue coat, with a black hat, and a black horse. He was sleepy again. But before he fell asleep on Mr Buffard's arm, he heard him say, "Mr Fletcher, a man at the inn told me Turpin was on Hounslow Heath last night, stopping the Bristol coach. If he tries to stop us . . . I'll . . ." But he did not say what he would do.

Peter wanted to know what he was going to say, but he couldn't make his eyes stay open. He slept.

A shout woke him up, a very big shout.

"Stand and deliver! Throw down your money!"

Peter saw a black horse standing on its back legs. With one hand, the rider tried to make it stand still. In his other hand he had a pistol. His face was covered with a cloth, but Peter knew the blue coat at once.

There was no time to say anything. The horse was standing still now, and the pistol looked very big in the highwayman's hand. "Get out of the coach, all of you!" he shouted.

They all stood in the road.

"The first person who moves," he called out again, "I shall shoot him dead."

Peter stood very still, and took his father's hand.

The horseman spoke to Mr Buffard.

"You, sir," he said, "you look very fat. Lots to eat, sir? Lots of money, eh? How many yellow-boys have you got for me?"

Now Mr Buffard had nothing to say.

"Can't speak, sir?" said the highwayman with a laugh. "If you don't speak soon, my pop here will speak." His fingers moved on the pistol.

"Please, sir," said Mr Buffard, "I have no money."

"I've heard that story before," was the answer. The pistol moved towards the fat man's head.

Buffard called out at once. "Don't shoot! Don't shoot! Here's my money!" And he took out a bag and gave it to the highwayman.

"I thank you, sir," said the horseman, with another laugh. "You're very kind. Are there any more of you who would like to be kind?"

Unhappily, the people from the coach gave him their money. Two had watches; some of them had gold rings. Simon Fletcher took out his little bag of money, looked at it sadly, and then gave it to the highwayman. But Simon said nothing.

"Is *this* Dick Turpin?" Peter thought. "Dick Turpin doesn't take poor men's money!"

Without thinking, Peter shouted at him. "My father has worked very hard for that money! You can't take it from us!"

Everyone looked at Peter.

"We're not rich, we're poor!"

The highwayman looked down at the boy. "Poor, are you, boy? I'm poor too."

"No, you're not, you're rich! I saw you at the Green Man. I saw your gold watch. And that blue coat is new!"

The highwayman looked angry and said, "Do you want me to shoot you? You know what this is, don't you, boy?"

Simon Fletcher spoke at last. "You would not shoot a child?"

The eyes under the cloth on the man's face moved to look at Simon. The pistol came up towards his head. Peter put his arms round his father's legs.

Then the highwayman laughed. "No, sir, you speak well. I would not! Dick Turpin doesn't shoot children! Remember that, boy! Tell your friends you've spoken to Turpin and you're still alive!"

He kicked his horse's sides, shouted, "Come on, Bess!" and rode into the trees. As he went, he threw something onto the ground.

Peter ran and got it. "Look, Father! Your money!"

Mr Buffard was very angry. "Why didn't he give mine back?" His face got red all over. "I had twenty pounds in my bag. Quick, get the constables!"

Written by Tony Barton
Illustrated by David Bone

The Tide Rises, the Tide Falls

The tide rises, the tide falls,
The twilight darkens, the curlew calls;
Along the sea-sands damp and brown,
The traveller hastens towards the town,
  And the tide rises, the tide falls.

Darkness settles on roofs and walls,
But the sea, the sea in the darkness calls;
The little waves, with their soft, white hands,
Efface the footprints in the sands,
  And the tide rises, the tide falls.

The morning breaks; the steeds in their stalls
Stamp and neigh, as the hostler calls;
The day returns, but nevermore
Returns the traveller to the shore,
  And the tide rises, the tide falls.

Henry Wadsworth Longfellow